unplugged

Steve Antony

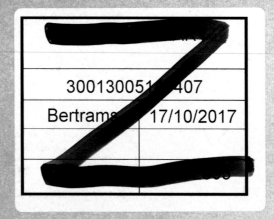

To Aiden, Annie and Eli

First published in Great Britain in 2017 by Hodder and Stoughton

Copyright © Steve Antony 2017

Hodder Children's Books
An imprint of Hachette Children's Group
Part of Hodder and Stoughton
Carmelite House
50 Victoria Embankment
London EC4Y 0DZ

HB ISBN 978 1 444 93415 1
PB ISBN 978 1 444 93416 8

1 3 5 7 9 10 8 6 4 2

Printed in China

An Hachette UK Company
www.hachette.co.uk

Hodder
Children's
Books

MIX
Paper from
responsible sources
FSC® C104740

Unplugged

Steve Antony

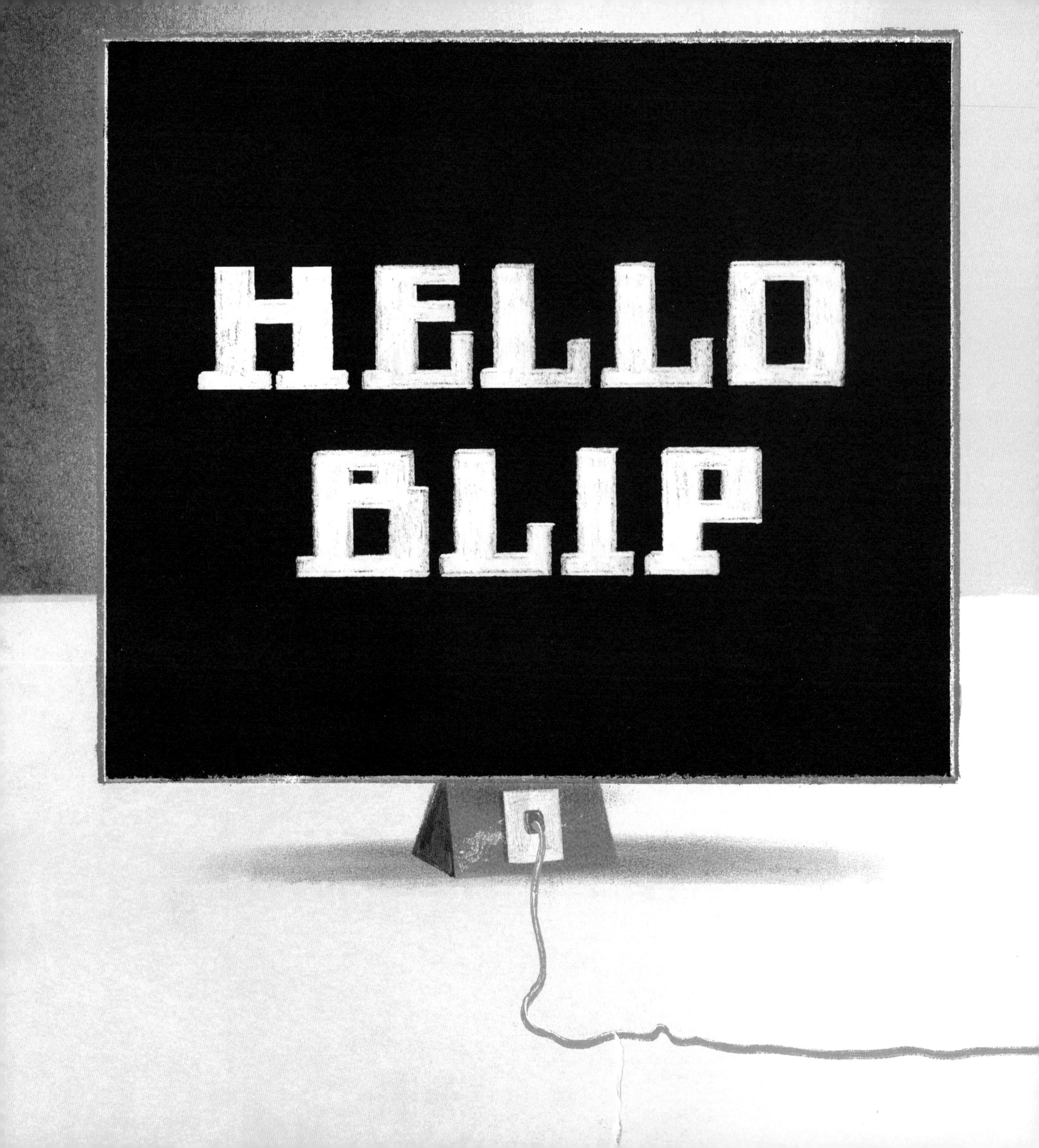
HELLO
BLIP

Blip liked being plugged
into her computer.

On her computer...

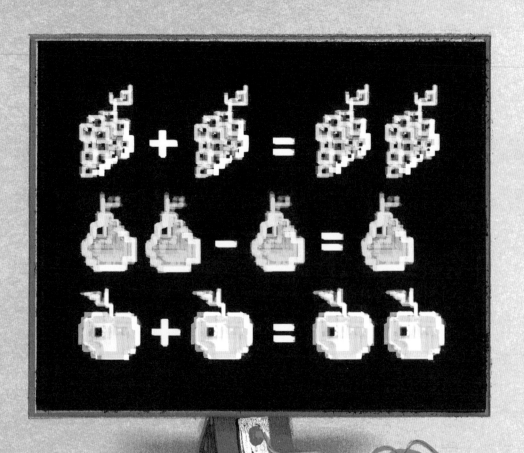

Blip learned
new things,

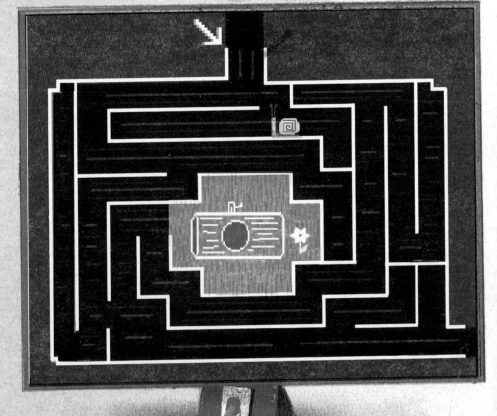

played fun games,

danced to music,

and visited
faraway places...

all day long.

But one day...

there was a POWER CUT!

And Blip tripped over her wire!

She tumbled...

all the way...

downstairs...

and out the front door.

Blip toppled
down a steep, grassy hill,

rolled through a forest of very tall trees,

and drifted down a long winding river.

Blip was outside.

Outside Blip learned new things,

played fun games,

danced to music,

and visited
faraway places...

all day...

long.

But it was getting late.

Blip sailed back up the long winding river,

and walked back through the forest of very tall trees,

and climbed back
up the steep,
grassy hill...

where she said goodbye
to her new friends.

upstairs...

all the way...

Blip walked...

and plugged back
into her computer.

Blip liked being plugged into her computer.
But all she could think about was...

how great it was...

to be...

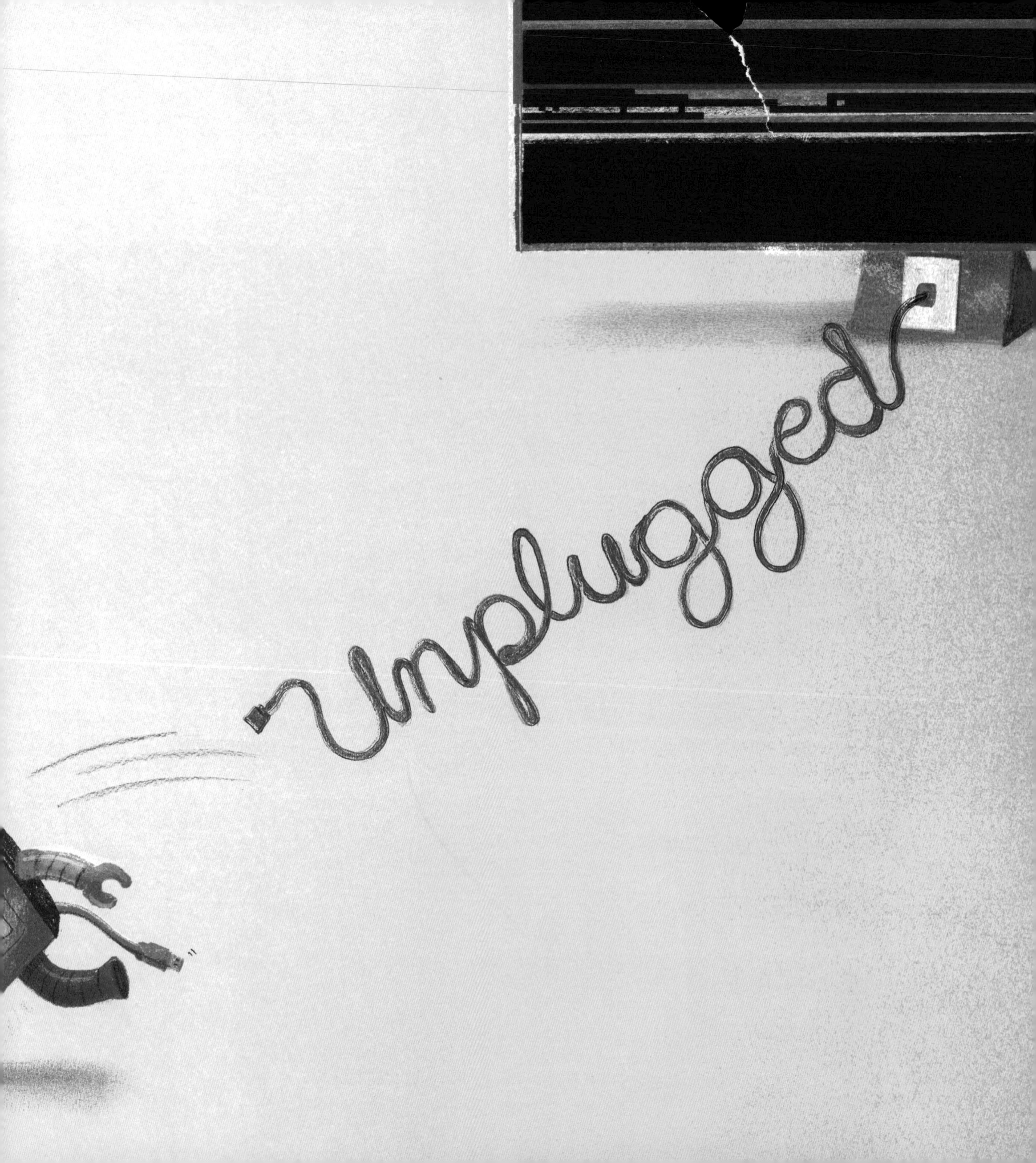
Unplugged

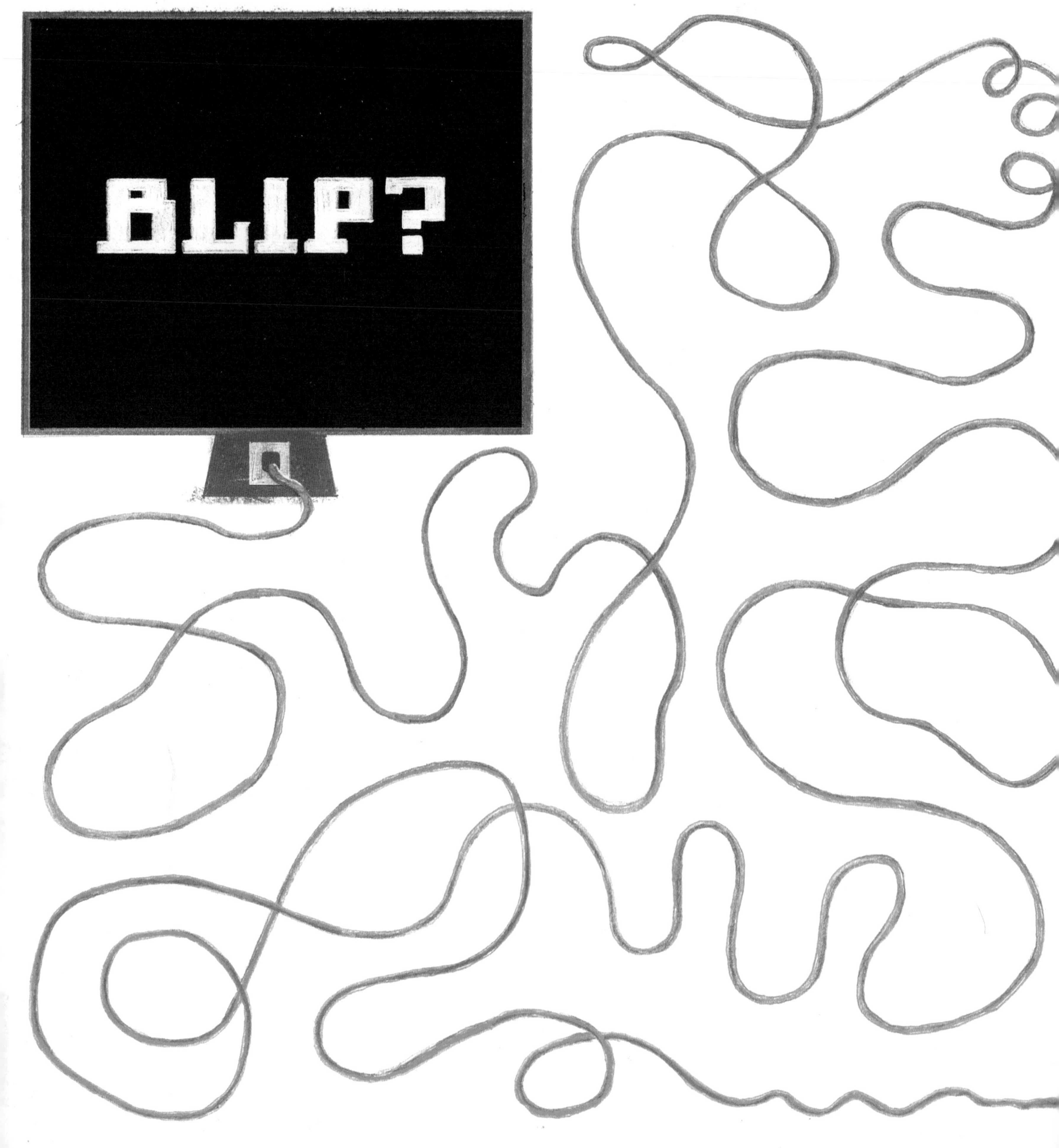
BLIP?